ABOUT THIS BOOK

Prepare to be amused by these five humorous fantasy stories involving dragons and slayers, deals with the Devil, 80s hair metal, and much, much more!

Praise for Dayle A. Dermatis

"Dayle A. Dermatis's 'If the Shoe Fits' is a funny (and rather ingenious) semi-modern twist on Cinderella, in which we find out why that shoe was really so important to everyone."

—Errant Dreams Reviews

"Dermatis has a love of lush language...."

– Tangent Online

Five Funny Fantasies
Dayle A. Dermatis

Ebook edition published 2024 by Soul's Road Press

"If the Shoe Fits" was originally published in *The Trouble With Heroes* (DAW Books, 2009).
"Feline Design" was originally published in *The Ghostbreakers: New Horrors* (Rage Machine Books, 2005).
"Hell's Belles" was originally published in *Deathgrip: Exit Laughing* (Hellbound Books, 2006).
"What Dragons Prefer" was originally published in *Marion Zimmer Bradley's Fantasy Magazine*, Fall 1994 (Issue 25). And if you want to hear it read aloud, head on over to Podcastle.org (2008)!

ISBN 978-1-946462-28-2

Inquiries should be addressed to
Soul's Road Press
info@soulsroadpress.com
http://www.soulsroadpress.com

Cover image © Julien Tromeur | iStockPhoto
Soul's Road Press logo: Designs by Trapdoor

FIVE FUNNY FANTASIES

DAYLE A. DERMATIS

SOUL'S
ROAD
PRESS

CONTENTS

IF THE SHOE FITS

When I heard the royal family would be holding a ball to find suitable wife material for the prince and heir, my mind went into overdrive.

But not in the way anyone would expect.

I didn't have specific information about how a royal household was run; I didn't know the number and skill sets of the servants, or even how many people would be invited to this shindig. But within ten minutes I had a pretty good sense of how much it would cost per person, even factoring in peacock meat (which seemed like a waste to me, what with chickens being that much cheaper per pound, but I also understood the art of entertaining sometimes meant being flashy to impress certain guests).

Not, mind you, that it was any of my business. Party planning wasn't really where I wanted to end up, but I loved the idea of it. Just the way my brain works: a challenge, a puzzle. I can put together a fundraising dinner and auction for 50 people without breaking a sweat. The concept of overseeing a royal ball made me go *squee* (on the inside).

Actually going to the ball? Meh. Marrying royalty didn't interest me in the least, and besides, I had finals coming up.

My aunt, Sheila, thought differently.

"It would be a good networking opportunity for you," she'd said.

"I'm not in the market for a husband," I'd said.

She'd rapped my knuckles with her wooden spoon, not enough to hurt, but it got my attention. "Don't be an idiot," she said. "I'm talking about *business* networking. You're about to graduate with honors. All those other girls giggling around the prince? Their daddies will be there, and their daddies run corporations that have job openings for the right candidates."

Oh. Duh. I'd been so busy helping my sisters not lose their freaking minds over the ball that it hadn't even occurred to me that this could be all about the schmoozing. Bad future entrepreneur, no BMW.

There's a reason why Aunt Sheila runs a thriving chain of bakeries.

Around me, young women clumped together, giggling (just as Aunt Sheila had predicted) and craning their necks to get a glimpse of Rupert, Prince Royal and Most Eligible Bachelor. I, on the other hand, had handed out a fair number of business cards, and was feeling rather smug.

Everybody says I work too hard. But I just cannot abide a disorganized house. After my mother died, my father...well, he was grieving, plus he had his own business to run, so the household fell to me. I was still young, but I wasn't stupid. I could clip coupons and plan a week's worth of simple, nutritious meals.

When my dad remarried, bringing not only a new wife into the house but also two new stepsisters for me, I suggested a rota of chores. Seemed only fair. They all laughed and went on gadding about.

So I just went on managing things. Oh, it was a PITA,

sure, but with more people in the house, *somebody* had to keep things running smoothly. Money was tight, but I was able to convince dad to let me hire a weekly cleaning lady so I had enough time to work on my degree in business management.

I was thinking about bailing and heading home to get some studying in when the crowd fell silent and parted, and there was Prince Rupert, handsome and dashing. He smiled, white teeth and dimples flashing, and the women around me gave a collective sigh.

Okay, he was a looker, I'll give him that. Piercing blue eyes, thick black hair, square jaw. Broad shoulders, slim hips. Almost a cliché.

He surveyed the people in this corner of the ballroom. I did my best to blend into the wallpaper. It would be the height of rudeness to sneak away, and I had a reputation to cultivate. With all the excitedly heaving bosoms around me, there was no way he'd notice...

Oh, *crap*. He was coming right for me.

He asked me to dance, and women who'd been mentally designing their wedding invitations glared daggers at me as we walked away.

"Your Highness," I said as soon as we were out of earshot of the crowd, "I'm honored by your interest, but I hope you'll allow me to speak plainly."

"Please," he said with a gracious nod of his head that struck me as a little too practiced.

Saying *I'm not interested in you* seemed a little blunt, so I explained that I didn't think I was princess material and that I had plans for a career and I was here largely to put those plans in motion. Only I said it much more politely and flowery.

"Well, I have to thank you for your honesty," he said. "When you first said you weren't princess material, it sounded like a line, but I think you really mean it. Believe me, that's refreshing. I've been desperate to talk to someone who has more on her mind than clinging to my every word and answering in a charming way that's designed to make me think she's The One."

It was quite a speech, let me tell you.

"If you want to find a potential wife tonight, you probably ought to be dancing with them, not me," I said.

"Protocol states I must give you the full dance," he said, "and I appreciate the chance to talk to someone interesting. Plus, I've been dying to ask you: Where did you get your shoes?"

My...huh? What?

Aunt Sheila had loaned them to me. She'd studied in Paris back in the day, and saved up her money for the one indulgence. I didn't know a shoe from a ship, but I knew these were exquisite, so-expensive-it-takes-your-breath-away pumps. They were, I knew, one of a kind, too—the burgundy silk and black lace were remnants, and no other pair had been made with the same fabrics.

I explained it all to Rupert (who was, I might mention, an incredibly good dancer).

"They really are fabulous," he said. "I wish I could get a better look at them. Would you like a drink?"

I blinked, recovered, and the next thing I knew we were in a private antechamber and I was drinking the best damn champagne on earth and he was turning one of my shoes over in his hands and examining the workmanship. He seemed to know what he was looking at.

He handed the pump back to me (I'd been afraid he'd gently replace it on my foot or something) and I slipped it on.

"You're so lucky," he said.

"Why?" I couldn't quite get that. He had the world at his fingertips, didn't he?

"You have choices," he said, "and the freedom to make

those choices. My path is set: marry a suitable woman, produce heirs, be the figurehead for a kingdom that already has a perfectly well-running government. The end."

Well...I'd never thought about that. "But there's some much you can do, with your connections and power. What about creating charities?"

"My future wife is expected to do that," he said. "Don't get me wrong, though—I do see those benefits. It's just that I'd give anything to have the freedom to pursue my own passions, live my own life." He waved a hand. "Oh, never mind."

I wanted to tell him to just go do whatever he bloody well wanted, because really, who was really going to protest? Wasn't his decree practically law?

Then I thought about it. I could very well have moved out and left the chaos of my family home behind me, giving me tons more time to move ahead with my own plans. But I felt a responsibility to them—just as Rupert must feel towards the kingdom.

So we talked about that, and I have to say, he was pretty easy to talk to. I kinda liked him, in a "I've never had a brother" sort of way.

His counselor peeking in the door made us both realize how long ago we'd ditched the ball, and made me realize just how late it was.

Crap.

There'd been no way in hell I could have driven there; the traffic was beyond a gridlocked nightmare. There wouldn't be any cabs. So if I didn't catch the last train, which left Palace Station just after midnight, I'd be stranded.

"Reallynicetalkingtoyou, gottago."

I grabbed my stuff from the coat check, laced on my sneakers (there was no way in hell I was going to commute in those stilettos, either), and made a mad dash to the train station.

It was only after I was sitting in the car and catching my breath that I realized I'd dropped one of the shoes somewhere along the way.

I said a word that *never* would have been appropriate in front of royalty.

<hr>

THANKFULLY AUNT SHEILA WAS OUT OF TOWN, SO I DIDN'T have to break the loss to her just yet. I was eyeballs-deep in finals over the next few days, pulling all-nighters at the library and crashing on a friend's sofa closer to the university, so I didn't hear about the whole ruckus until I stumbled home.

"Where have you been; I've left messages," my stepmom said.

I pulled out my cell. Yep, there were messages. Who knew?

"The palace has been looking for you." She twisted her hands together. "We were hoping they were calling about Genna or Clara."

"It's just about my shoe," I said. "I dropped it when I was leaving. I'm sure they just want to return it."

But even I wondered why they couldn't have just popped it into the mail, you know?

So I called back, and was put on hold forever (royal Muzak is no better than your local bank's, believe me) before someone got back on the line and told me that Prince Rupert would like to return the shoe to me personally and was I free for a private dinner at the palace tomorrow?

That just didn't bode well. I'd caught up on the news and knew that the prince hadn't selected a prospective wife (or even a short list of candidates) since the ball. I couldn't imagine Rupert taking the time to hang out with me when he had bigger fish to fry...unless it was my fish he had an interest in.

Had I not made myself clear? Had *he* not made himself clear?

But I had to get that shoe back before Aunt Sheila got home.

I had a private audience with the prince in the "small" dining room, which was almost the size of my father's house. At least we weren't at opposite ends of the table that yawned the length of the room. If we had, we'd've needed walkie-talkies.

We made small talk through the soup course, and then he leaned forward and said, "Ella."

His tone of voice made me vaguely itchy. I doubted I'd like what he had to say. "Your Highness."

"I have a business proposition for you."

Oh. Well, then. I sat forward. "I'm always interested in that."

"I need a wife."

I sat back. "I don't—"

"Please, hear me out." He looked almost as unhappy as I felt, so I let him continue. "I've met many fine women, so many who would be appropriate for the role of princess. But I have some...special requirements, and I don't believe any of those women would understand or agree to them."

Great. He had a kinky streak.

"Those women are looking for a great romance, and that's something I can never give them," he continued.

Oh. A mistress, then, someone he could never put on the throne.

But no. He kept going. "You have other goals in life, ones that I can facilitate. I think we can both benefit from a joint venture."

He went on to detail what I'd get out of the deal, which included some pretty nifty corporate responsibilities. In return, I'd be his wife essentially in name only, and he'd be able to pursue his personal passions, as he'd called them.

The pre-nup included a confidentiality agreement, and when I read it, it was like a blinding light going off over my head. All of the signs had been there, but like everyone else, I just hadn't put them together.

His disinterest in the sea of heaving bosoms. His fascination with my fabulous shoes....

SO THERE YOU HAVE IT. RUPERT REMAINS THE COUNTRY'S figurehead, and designs shoes and handbags (and occasionally hats) under a fake name. He's quite good; his latest line got a huge write-up in *Vogue*. We pay a private physician handsomely to keep quiet about the artificial insemination to get me pregnant. (Yeah, I've always focused on getting a career, but I never said kids were out of the question.)

And me? I get to be CFO of Rupert's design firm *and* manage the royal finances, and for fun I throw elaborate, glittering dinner parties and fundraisers for up to a thousand people.

Squee.

Author's Note

I WROTE "IF THE SHOE FITS" FOR AN ANTHOLOGY CALLED The Trouble With Heroes. What happens when the hero comes back from storming the castle? If you're the damsel he rescued...well, now what? That opened up so many fun ideas!

I confess I can't remember the thought process I went through to come up with the story. I clearly recall, though, that at one point in the story, it could've gone two ways. I can't tell you what the other one is without spoiling the story...but can you guess?

"If the Shoe Fits" appeared *The Trouble With Heroes* (DAW Books, 2009).

FELINE DESIGN

The police radio crackled, spitting instructions, but Miranda Contreau ignored them. She was already on the way to her assignment, and it was important enough—and she was high-ranking enough—that no other emergency would take precedence. Her backup team awaited her at the scene.

She steered the BMW through the winding Glenwood streets with determination but not urgency; the crime had already been committed. The streets were mostly deserted, the residents of the upper-middle-class Los Angeles suburb apartments at work on this sunny midweek afternoon. Miranda didn't bother glancing at the paper on her dashboard to compare the address to the numbers painted on the curb: the black-and-white cars fanned around the flapping yellow police tape told her when she reached the right place.

From the rear-view mirror she pulled off a chain and looped it around her left wrist. Various silver charms—cross, pentagram, Star of David, yin yang, raven—tinkled as she checked the gun at her waist, which was inscribed with the same symbols. Miranda wasn't a particularly religious woman, but this murder seemed to be the next in a gruesome series, and even if the symbolism of the icons didn't have personal meaning for her, the murderer would respect at least one of them.

Demons were funny that way.

She got out of the car and kicked through the drying palm fronds on the sidewalk, victims of a recent storm. Sergeant Georgiou opened the door before Miranda reached the top step of the apartment.

"Heard you drive up, Lieutenant," he greeted. "You still haven't gotten that transmission fixed."

"I've narrowed the language down to Farsi, but not the specific imp," she replied. "If you don't stop bugging me about it, Adam, I'm going to assign *you* to research the native gremlins of Iran. Now, show me the body."

He led the way into the apartment. In less stressful circumstances, she would have admired his lean-hipped physique beneath the standard-issue tan polyester, not to mention his dark Mediterranean features that were charmingly marred by a chipped front tooth. Instead, she drew her gun. Sometimes demons came back to admire their handiwork.

The building had been built in the Thirties and retained much of its charisma outside. The inside hadn't fared too badly, having been subdivided into only two apartments where many other contractors would have squeezed out four. The apartments were narrow and tall, three stories plus basement. Adam started down the hall, but Miranda paused, moving left halfway into the kitchen.

It was deceptively spacious, bisected by a counter with glass doors on both sides. From a copper rack above dangled an assortment of polished pots, and herbs grew in a planter on the broad windowsill. As an amateur chef, Miranda envied the tenant that kitchen, its airy light and its sleek silver

KitchenAid mixer. But the half-cooked bacon in a pan on the stove reminded her that envy was useless when the object of envy had been eviscerated.

Something brushed against her ankle and she jumped back, both gun and bracelet aimed down. She heard a chuckle.

"The place is swarming with them," Adam said from the doorway as the cat, unimpressed with Miranda's reaction, sauntered over and rubbed against the sergeant's leg instead.

"You're sure they're cats?"

He looked a trifle sheepish. "Well, yeah, you see, when we got here they were out of food, and I fed them before I thought about that. They all chowed right down, though."

Miranda saw the six double-bowls lined up against the far baseboard. All bore signs of recent dining.

"There haven't been any indications that the perpetrator in these murders is feline," she said. "Since they all ate cat food, I'd guess they're safe. You saw all of them?"

"All six," he confirmed. "There are kittens upstairs, too."

"Six." Miranda pondered for a moment. "Possibly a correlation there. Have Lennox review all the murder sites and see if there's a pattern with the number six."

He nodded, and this time she followed him to the basement door. "You might want to hold your breath," he suggested. "We put a confinement bubble at the top of the stairs 'cause it's pretty bad down there."

His warning helped, but the stench still made her pause, swallowing rapidly, after she moved through the shield that was keeping the odor from entering the rest of the house.

Forensics was already there, the photographer snapping away at different angles. Ironically, the dead woman had been a model. Now the only thing she could advertise were the benefits of cremation.

Miranda chatted briefly with forensics, who confirmed

her visual estimate that the same perpetrator had almost certainly committed the other murders. The woman had been cleanly slit from neck to groin with an implement that cauterized the edges of the cut. Miranda stepped delicately around a curl of small intestines on her way back up the stairs.

The rest of the apartment was tastefully furnished, artfully decorated, and empty of helpful clues. Miranda worked her way through the rest of the ground floor (living room, dining room, downstairs half bath), second floor (two bedrooms, one converted into a study, and full bath), and third floor (apparently originally the attic, it had been left open and had skylights installed, and was being used as a photography studio). On her way back down, she stopped again in the master bedroom. She tried to tell herself that it was because she was unable to resist a second peek at the basket on the bed, filled with a jumble of peacefully napping kittens.

She suspected that it wasn't the only reason. There was a *wrongness* here—faint, but distinct. It was minor enough that she'd let it go the first time, but since she hadn't found anything else, this was worth double-checking.

As she watched, a grey-striped ball of fluff disentangled itself from its brethren. Several of the other kittens mewled half-hearted protests, not even bothering to open their eyes. The grey kitten yawned, revealing tiny chips of pointed ivory. It stretched, then put its paws up on the side of the basket and blinked wide orange eyes at Miranda.

The murder was almost stripped from her mind. She could still smell the aroma of wrongfully exposed innards; it would be trapped in her nostril hairs for the rest of the day, or at least until she found some rose geranium essential oil. But for a moment, she could push the thoughts aside, not focus on the unsolved string of deaths and the lack of obvious connecting factors that would at least explain the type of demon they were dealing with. For a moment, she just wanted to get mushy over a basket of petite kittens with fur like angel-hair. She sighed.

She'd replaced the her gun in its holster after she searched the house. Now, she simply raised her left hand, brandishing the charm bracelet, as she re-searched this room on a different level, with different sight.

Miranda grounded and centered, pulling energy from the earth. She slowly walked around the room, clockwise, jingling the bracelet and causing the small bell on it to chime. The ring would sound different—probably duller—if it encountered any trapped energy. Trapped energy didn't mean evil energy, but it was a start.

The experiment failed. The owner had used good Feng Shui techniques.

She stroked the pale slate kitten on the top of its head with one finger, and it playfully batted at the dangling charms, stretching its tiny paw wide. Miranda chuckled, overwhelmed by the adorableness of it—it had six toes on each of its front paws.

Finally, with a sigh, she turned away, making a mental note to have Lennox call the SPCA.

She leaned against the doorjamb to the bedroom, reviewing all the facts she knew about the case. The previous murders. The eviscerated woman in the basement. The way the half-prepared food in the kitchen smelled, the way the light streamed in through the skylights. The house number, the street name, the architecture. Mentally she walked through the house, again and again.

Miranda was about to head downstairs when it hit her.

The kitten, still clinging to the side of the basket, watched her, unblinking.

"You're the Antichrist, aren't you?"

Very deliberately, the kitten nodded.

Miranda took a deep breath, let it out. "And even if I destroy that form you're in, it won't destroy you."

The kitten shook its head from one side to the other.

"Well, hell." Hands on her hips, Miranda stared at the kitten. Then the ridiculousness of her last words struck her, and she burst out laughing.

Sergeant Georgiou met her in the downstairs hall. "Everything okay?" he asked. "I heard maniacal laughter."

Any other time, she would have threatened to dock his pay. Instead, as she hurried by him, she said, "I think I may have figured all this out. I have to go to the Lab. I'll keep you posted."

The last words were over her shoulder as she left the apartment. Let Adam try to figure out why there was a kitten in her breast pocket.

SATAN WAS MOSTLY QUIET DURING THE RIDE. IN THE kitten body, he couldn't make any sound other than ones that cats normally made, so Miranda made no attempt to communicate with him. She laid her charm bracelet on the centre console for extra protection, even though it hadn't stopped him before, but he didn't try to cross the barrier. Instead, he curled on the passenger seat and napped, tail wrapped around his body to cover his little pink nose, one paw across his eyes.

He didn't awaken when Miranda slowed marginally, holding her badge out the window for the security guard at the Lab grounds' main gate as she approached. Officers often had to get through the gates—the physical aspect that indicated where the spell wards had been placed—as fast as possible, and the guards were aware of that. The metal barrier swung open, and Miranda spoke the charm that would allow her car and its contents through without breaking a hole in the magickal field. Satan roused as she stamped the accelerator, alerted by either the sudden change in speed, the wards, or both, but by then it was too late. They had crossed through, and he was on the Lab grounds, the most secure place on earth for containing and suppressing negative supernatural activity.

Still, he didn't seem to care. Miranda watched him out of the corner of her eye as she slid the BMW into her parking spot in front of the Lab's main building. Made of concrete, edged with darker grey blocks, it looked more like the outside of a seedy movie studio than a technologically advanced centre for dealing with the paranormal. Satan didn't seem overly concerned; in fact, he was studiously going through the pattern of licking his right paw, swiping it behind his right ear, and repeating. It was probable, Miranda knew, that the wards had no effect on him. He was one of the most powerful beings imagined by man (so far, at any rate) and the containment spells here had been designed to deter demons, witches, vampires, and the like.

But none of those beings could hold a candle to the Antichrist.

She entered the building, passing through the scanner. To her surprise, Satan registered only as a cat. In some ways, it was logical: He wasn't a demon or witch or evil spirit, all of which the scanner was set to identify. But it also served to prove his power. Miranda shivered as the retinal scan identified her, allowing her access to the main part of the building. She hoped she wasn't in over her head.

Satan roused himself enough to peer out of her pocket. He yawned, wider than it seemed a kitten's mouth could go, then settled back, contented, sleepy.

As she walked towards the containment facilities, a sergeant came up beside her, matching her long stride.

"Lieutenant Contreau, what facilities do you require?" The woman handed her a wireless headset, and Miranda fitted it over her head, adjusting the microphone comfortably in front of her face.

"The main sealant room, and every able-bodied person stationed outside of it to cast a major religious barrier. All religions that we have access to, though Christian's most crucial. I think."

If the other woman—Anna O'Grady, Miranda saw from her nametag—was concerned by the need for the big guns, she gave no sign; nor did she react to the kitten in Miranda's breast pocket.

"Med team?" The smaller woman doubled her stride to keep up.

The medical team could provide a number of injections and drugs to pacify or knock out every demon they'd encountered so far, and probably a few new ones. Miranda shook her head. Not likely.

"What about backup?" Anna asked, adjusting her own microphone, which currently communicated their conversation and Miranda's requirements throughout the station.

Miranda tensed again; forced herself to relax, release the negative energy. "Don't bother. If the initial spell doesn't work, then we're toast, I'm afraid."

Anna did blanch at that, although to her credit, she had no other reaction. "Noted," she said. "Anything else?"

"I'll need a spell to give voice to mute creatures. That's it."

"Good luck, Lieutenant," the sergeant said, and peeled off as Miranda turned the corner and headed down the internal corridor towards the containment facilities.

The empty, warehouse-like room had titanium-steel walls and floor. Various inscriptions and symbols covered the smooth surfaces, invoking protection and confinement and magickal dampening; pentacles and triskeles, a consoling

Jesus and a contented Buddha, the moon in her splendor and the sun in his. If those failed, various cages of bars or sound or electricity, or any combination, could be dropped from the ceiling.

"East," Miranda said.

Somehow, she could sense everyone outside the room turning east. Some called on the spirit of fire. Others dropped to their knees and pressed their foreheads against the ground, connecting to Mecca. Others simply thought of God.

"South."

The pagans invoked the spirits of earth, or fire, depending on their particular bent. The Muslims stayed facing east. The Christians and Jews may have turned, automatically, but they still invoked their God. Everyone was in harmony.

"West."

Water. The Native Americans increased the intensity of their drumming.

Energy swelled; Miranda could feel it tingling around her, like air before a lightning strike. She continued to light the candles in a circle around herself and the kitten. Circles within circles. She had to believe they would help. Lack of belief meant automatic failure.

"North."

Air or Earth. The outer circle closed, with assistance from every religious denomination. It wouldn't be easy for Satan to break the seal. However, Miranda didn't for a moment think it would be impossible for him to do so. She lit the final candle, and glanced up at the wall, where the crucified Jesus stared down at them with pitying brown eyes. She grounded, gathering strength from whatever sources supplied it.

Into her headset, she requested the spell to give the ability of speech. She didn't recognize the language, but she carefully repeated each syllable as she heard it.

An emerald flare of energy lined the circle, then dissipated, as she finished.

"Well, this is interesting."

His voice was several octaves in one, neither male nor female, but at the same time, both genders.

"Makes communication a little easier," Miranda explained. "This way, I'm not stuck with yes-or-no questions."

"So." He looked around the room. "Remarkable set-up you have here."

"Thank you."

He cocked his head at her, lifted his left paw and licked it, then swiped behind his ear. "I have to ask: How did you guess it was Me?"

Miranda smiled, suppressing a flash of pride (he'd want that). "Six cats in the house, six kittens, a kitten with six toes. 666, the Number of the Beast. Plus this was the sixth murder, and the house was in the 600 block. There are probably more correlations, but the tip-off was your toes."

It was strange to hear a deep rumbling laugh out of the tiny kitten, especially a laugh that jittered through Miranda's bones. "I continue to be impressed," Satan said.

"I'm not sure what the rules are here, but can I demand an answer for an answer?"

He considered that. "A fair trade. I'll abide by the rules so far."

"Why this form?" Miranda asked. "The modus operandi under which we were searching gave no indication of a feline perp—although in that small form, you couldn't have torn apart the women anyway, so I have to assume the kitten body is a later addition. But why?"

"That's your question? Not why the women were eviscerated, or whether there really is a Heaven and Hell, or the true facts behind My fall from grace? You want to know why I chose a kitten's body?"

Miranda considered. The other questions were tempting. But she had a feeling that no matter why he was eviscerating women, he'd still keep doing it if he so chose. As for the religious matters, she wasn't necessarily Christian, so they hadn't really occurred to her. Her boss might rail at her later, but her job wasn't to interview the perpetrators, just to track and either destroy them or bring them in. If her superior wanted theological dialogue, he needed to send in the interrogation team.

What she wanted to know—what she thought might be important—she would ask.

"Sorry to disappoint you," she said. "But yes, that's my question."

"Convenience," he said. "Plain and simple. Not the earth-shattering confession you were looking for, eh? The fact is, I got tired. I was tired, and I needed—what do you call it?—down time. The kitten was a convenient host. What else gets to sleep more than a six-week-old kitten? Plus, I thought, no interruptions, no demands on my time... A little petting and cuddling I can suffer through. The rest of it is my own time: sleeping, eating, and then sleeping again."

His answer was so bizarre that it took Miranda a moment to process it all. She shook her head to clear it. "You were *tired?*"

The kitten—Satan in a kitten's body—yawned again. "I'm afraid so. Does that destroy all your assumptions about Me? If so, I could probably shift into a different body and cause some mayhem, to prove it's really Me."

"That's quite all right," Miranda said hastily. "I'm in the business of preventing mayhem, you see."

Satan somehow managed to give the impression of shrugging. "Fair enough. Too bad, really. I could use someone with your quick responses."

"I suppose I should be flattered."

"You should be."

They fell silent for a moment. Miranda could feel the thrumming of energy at the edges of the room. Would it give her any protection if he got angry?

"I'm a little scared to ask this," Miranda said finally, "but what are you going to do with me now? I know your secret. The kitten form's not safe anymore. Even if you went into a different kitten body, my team would still try and track you down."

"I confess, I'm not particularly concerned with you or your team," Satan said. "I *can* take over a different animal form, or a human one, or retreat to my...domain—but even that has its burdens, which I'm trying to avoid right now." He rolled over on his back, from paws curled against his white-furred chest. "To answer your unasked but entirely obvious question: Yes, I could break through the barriers here. They're quite impressive, I'll give you that—it would take some effort. But I could do it."

Miranda's heart thudded in her chest. She hoped he couldn't read her mind.

"What if I offered you a deal?"

"What deal could you possibly offer me?" His tone was nonchalant, almost sarcastic. But he rolled back over and sat up.

"Sanctuary. A place and opportunity to rest."

Again, that eerie, rumbling laugh, which didn't belong to that small body. "Why would you do that?"

Miranda took a deep breath. "Sympathy, I guess. You deserve rest just like anyone else. But don't get me wrong: It's selfish as well. While you're resting, you can't be wreaking havoc here on earth. That'll make my job—our job—that much easier for awhile.

"There would have to be some ground rules, of course. You'll stay as a cat for the duration of its natural lifetime.

Absolutely no evil-doing while you're in that form. For all intents and purposes, you'll be a cat. No powers beyond that of a normal cat."

He lifted a hind leg abruptly and licked. That seemed to take all the time he needed, because when he lowered the leg he said, "I accept. It's a deal."

Miranda had expected more wrangling, more attempt at loopholes from the Lord of Lies. Everything she had studied in the past about Satan had showed that he would never break a contract—although he usually added a clause that would trip up the unwary human who signed. "You—you accept? All the terms?"

"Seems easy enough. Besides, I'm hungry." He looked around the room. "I don't see any kibble in the immediate vicinity, and you're the most convenient person to supply it. Except I don't want kibble—canned food, if you please. And those fishy-shaped soft treats."

IN THE END, THEY COMPROMISED ON ONE MORE THING: Miranda could hear what he was thinking, and respond in kind, mentally. Many people believed cats were telepathic, so it could be argued that it wasn't beyond normal cat powers.

She was regretting that part of the deal by the time they left PetSmart.

The veterinary section had an opening, so she left him there while she shopped, ignoring his protests (as she'd expected) when she told the vet that his name was Cuddles. Her bank balance was going to take quite a hit, she mused as she walked through the aisles, filling her cart with food (including fishy-shaped soft treats), toys, and a scratching post. She was considering the merits of clay litter versus the clumping kind when the tirade began.

His commentary during vaccination was one thing; his howls of protest, heard only by Miranda, while the vet checked his temperature, were another...

The diatribe continued out to the car, while she loaded the food, litter, tray and scoop, and other purchases into the trunk. She buckled his carrier into the passenger seat and started the car. Turning on the air conditioning, she sighed with relief as the cold air washed over her.

"Listen to me," she said aloud. "You are a cat. You agreed to be a normal cat for its lifetime. Meanwhile, I am a responsible cat owner. Responsible cat owners make sure their pets have regular checkups and inoculations. I don't want you getting sick, or dying before your time. Besides," she added, "you think that back there was bad? Just wait 'til you're old enough to be spayed."

The mental image she got was of him flinging himself under the wheels of a car.

"Uh-uh," she said, waving a finger in front of the plastic grille of his cage. "The agreement is that you'd stay in that form for its natural lifetime. Cats don't commit suicide—it's not innate for them, so you can't do that." She pulled the car out onto the street and headed out of LA, towards the Valley and home. "If you're lucky, maybe that cat's body is destined to die young, from a tumor or honest accident."

She smirked. "But don't forget: Cats have nine lives. I think we'll be together for quite some time."

Author's Note

ONE DAY MY FRIEND AMANDA TOLD ME ABOUT A DREAM she'd had the night before, involving kittens and Satan. I remember scribbling it down, telling her it was going to be a story...and that's where "Feline Design" was born. What more can I say?

Miranda Contreau clearly wanted to be a series character, and along with "The Enemy of My Enemy's Blood" (which I haven't yet sold at the time of this writing), I have several other ideas for her. Hm. Seems like I should write them and do another collection!

"Feline Design" appeared in *The Ghostbreakers: New Horrors* (Rage Machine Books, 2005).

FAMOUS LAST WORDS

This meeting will now come to order."

Robert's Rules of Orders always ran the meetings. That was its job. It could get pretty officious, but most of the other books didn't mind too much.

Pages rustled and whispered as the paperbacks gathered in the little sunken amphitheatre in the children's area of the store. The hardcovers bumped and thumped their way along, slow and steady, spines creaking. The trade paperbacks—redheaded stepchildren that they were—settled in their own area.

"We're here to discuss the same issue as last time, and hopefully move closer to a solution," *Robert's Rules* said. "Today we have a guest speaker, *Publisher's Weekly*, to update us on the crisis."

"Thank you. Latest statistics show e-book sales tripling each month," the magazine said. "And at Amazon dot com, e-book sales have finally surpassed print sales."

The resulting uproar had *Robert's Rules* shouting for order again.

"It's a bleeping nightmare," said the latest Nora Robert's novel (nobody could keep track which one—there seemed to be a new one at every meeting) in its gravelly, smoker's voice.

"Pages will be come irrelevant, just like tracks on records did."

"And sides," *Rolling Stone's Guide to Music* said mournfully. "Remember when you had to flip an LP or cassette over? Sides meant something then. Now it's just mp3 this, mp3 that, blah blah blah. There's no *structure* anymore."

"We're all going to be relegated to the Great Remaindered Warehouse in the Sky!" every Shakespearean tragedy wailed like a Greek chorus.

"Oh, *please*," a pretentious literary novel said. "You're overreacting. It's all just a metaphor for the human condition."

"As in, print books being replaced by e-books means that humans are going to be replaced by robots?" asked the Asimov novel.

The pretentious literary novel sniffed and edged away from the Asimov, as if by removing itself from the genre book's presence it would maintain its aloof superiority.

The genre novels quietly snickered over their own better sales and popularity. The romance novels were especially smug.

Publisher's Weekly went on. "Sales of the Kindle are estimated to have been eight million units last year."

A Dr. Seuss book piped up, "I do not want to be in a Kindle. I do not want to..." It trailed off.

"What's wrong?" *Chicken Soup for the Soul* asked in a soothing tone.

"The only thing that rhymes with 'Kindle' is 'spindle,' and that doesn't fit."

"What about 'swindle'?" a rhyming dictionary asked.

"Ooh!" the Dr. Seuss book said, and wandered off to contemplate how to work that in.

"I remember when things were written on stone tablets," the Bible intoned. "Stone tablets! Authors really had to think about what they were going to say then!"

Almost everyone else ignored it. Given that all its prophesizing about Revelations hadn't come to pass, they didn't put much stock in its words anymore.

"Shut up, you old fart," the Nora Roberts book couldn't keep from muttering.

"Moreover, with the latest Nook coming out from Barnes & Noble and e-reader technology advancing every day..."

Publisher's Weekly didn't have time to finish before *Neuromancer* cried out, "Oh my God! What if they end up downloading books directly to their brains!?"

The place exploded into an uproar again, and *Robert's Rules* wished it came packaged with a gavel. It was surprised nobody got shredded into confetti or spontaneously combusted. (It kept an eye on *Firestarter* just in case.)

When it could be heard above the din again, it shouted, "Books! Pull yourselves together! Don't break your bindings!" The chaos subsided into urgent murmuring, and *Robert's Rules* continued. "We know there's a crisis. The world as we know it—the world of print books—will come to an end unless we do something about it. We need solutions, not panic. Anyone have any proactive suggestions? Yes, *War and Peace*, you have the floor."

"I say we attack."

"Typical," said an erotic romance. "Haven't you ever heard of 'make love, not war'? I say we seduce them."

"That's going a little above and beyond, I think," the Nora Roberts novel said. "But a good relationship *is* all about respect and communication. I think we should negotiate."

Pride and Prejudice made a witty, cutting remark. The Nora Roberts novel flipped a middle page at it.

"If a crime has been committed," said *A is for Alibi* (or maybe it was *B is for Burglar*; they were always next to each other), "then we need to hire our best detectives to find the perpetrator and bring him to justice!"

The entire Nancy Drew series and every single damn one of Robert B. Parker's books nodded in assent.

The Clive Cussler novels banded together and suggested wildly improbable things that still sounded like a page-turning ride, while the collection of Ian Flemings added that there should be infiltration using high-tech gadgets, followed by hot tubbing with at least three supermodel autobiographies.

"You know, there's an actual good idea in there," *The Art of War* commented. "Infiltrating their ranks would give us a better understanding of their goals and methods—we might even be able to get our covers on their plans for world domination."

"We have a motion on the floor," *Robert's Rules* said. "Do we have a second?"

In the end, it was agreed that a team of *The Complete Idiot's Guide to the Internet* and *E-Book Publishing Success* would sneak in and do reconnaissance at amazon.com, smashwords.com, and eharlequin.com (even though *E-Book Publishing Success* was feared by some to be a potential double-agent. "Keep your enemies closer," *Bartlett's Quotations* whispered.).

The *Twilight* series continued to sulk in the corner, still pissed off over its latest sequel being leaked early to the Internet and then canceled by its author.

THEY GATHERED AGAIN, CALLED TOGETHER UNEXPECTEDLY. *Robert's Rules* hopped up on the counter of cash registers to be better heard.

"Shouldn't we wait for the reconnaissance team to get back?" someone asked.

"This is an emergency interim meeting," *Robert's Rules* explained. "A special order has come in that could be picked up soon, and we think it could give us some very valuable information."

The remaining group voted to hear what the new book had to say.

"Thank you," said *A Short History of the Printed Word*. "I know my time here is limited. I just wanted to give you my take on the situation.

"There was a crisis when Gutenberg invited the printing press. Although it did allow the greater dissemination of information, printing didn't make handwriting or calligraphy go away. It even boosted the ability of people to become authors in their own right.

"There was a crisis when the computer became a common household object. Would authors spend less time editing? Would self-publishing destroy New York? But books—and good writing—didn't go away."

The pretentious literary novel yawned. *Good Night Moon* fell asleep in the corner, its front cover resting on *The Yearling*'s spine.

"And now there's a crisis over e-books," *A Short History of the Printed Word* went on. "But don't you see the pattern? People won't stop writing—or reading."

"But what will happen to *us*?" every Shakespearean tragedy wanted to know. "It'll be the end of *us*! Print books are *doomed*!"

"You're a history book," the Asimov novel pointed out. "You're not qualified to forecast or ruminate on the future.

That's what science fiction is for." Its entire section rustled in agreement.

"Oh, right," the Bible said. "Like you always get it right. Where are the flying cars, precisely?"

"Pot, meet kettle," the Asimov novel shot back.

Before the discussion could completely degenerate into a heated debate between genres, *Robert's Rules* hastily thanked *A Short History of the Printed Word* for its insightful comments and adjourned the meeting.

The Complete Idiot's Guide to the Internet and *E-Book Publishing Success* finally came limping back, their covers bent and their pages limp from their time in the field. But they had an aura of optimism about them.

They hauled over the latest *Publisher's Weekly*, since it had updated information as well, and gave their report.

They'd gone to the three sites as assigned, but also to many others—where, they revealed, they'd been greeted as cousins and comrades in arms.

"The atmosphere is one of solidarity and sharing," they said. "E-books have no interest in replacing us!"

"How is that possible?" asked *Robert's Rules*, speaking out of order in astonishment.

"People buy both print books and e-books, just as they buy mass market, trade, and hardcover! It depends on the book! In fact, if an e-book and a hardcover are the same price, they'll choose the hardcover!"

"Damn straight," the Nora Roberts novel (possibly yet another new one; nobody was entirely sure) said.

"Even more amazing: if an e-book is offered for free, many readers will *still* go out and purchase it at the hardcover price if they liked it," they went on. "They want it for their shelves."

"Plus there are people who simply prefer the feel and format of a print book," *Publisher's Weekly* said.

"I'm glad to hear there is no hell," the Dr. Seuss book said. "I will not throw myself down a well."

"It's still change," every Shakespearean tragedy whined. "I don't *like* it."

"Suck it up," the Nora Roberts novel growled, "or I'll sic the nuns on you."

"Speaking of change," *Robert's Rules* said, "can we move on to the next agenda item? We really have to address the genocidal practice of returns again."

———

Author's Note

FOR A NUMBER OF YEARS I'VE ATTENDED A WORKSHOP IN Oregon taught by a editor who worked for Tekno Books (which no longer exists). A book packager, Tekno were the folks that come up with the ideas for all those nifty DAW fantasy and SF anthologies (among many other projects). At the workshops, attendees were given the chance to write stories for upcoming anthologies.

"Famous Last Words" was written for an anthology theme that didn't get picked up at DAW: the end of the world as we know it. It's a pretty open theme, when you think about it. The end of the world doesn't have to mean earth blowing up. It's the end of the character's world as s/he knows it. A dog's world pretty much ends every time their owner walks out the door without them.

The year we got this theme was just before the tipping point when electronic books started to take off. We'd all been discussing the coming changes in some depth, so when I went to write the story, that's what popped into my head: For print books, electronic books meant the end of the world as they knew it.

I laughed and laughed the entire time I wrote this, which was kind of weird because my roommate was writing a dark story and sniffling in the far corner. (Sorry, Phae.) I confess I still snort every time I read it. I hope you snicker, too.

HELL'S BELLES

Rich Southern women have had common sense bred right out of them. What's replaced it is an overdeveloped obsession with ritual and decorum, and a fear of looking bad in society.

Which isn't a terrible thing, because it keeps me in a job.

I'm the most sought-after debutante trainer in the South. Mothers may think their daughters are perfect, having had exquisite training at exclusive finishing schools, but those girls have nothing if they haven't had my attention. And every socialite south of the Mason-Dixon Line knows it.

I had one woman faint dead away when I told her I was already booked for the season. When she came to, she offered me three times my fee (which is already considerable). I agreed only with the stipulation that she not tell my first client that I was training two girls that season.

Of course the first thing she did was blab. But it violated her contract—it was right there, in black and white, and she'd signed it—so in the end it all worked out just fine for me.

This season, I would be responsible for the social graces and elegance of one Miss Alexandria (never to be called

Alex) Pointer-Ashe. The Pointer-Ashe home was pure Antebellum, with fat white columns framing the front door. On the side porch, we would no doubt sip mint juleps while Mrs. Margaret Pointer-Ashe and her daughter signed my contract.

I handed my card to the meek-looking maid who answered the door. "Lilith D'Enfer to see Mrs. Pointer-Ashe and Miss Alexandria Pointer-Ashe," I said as she glanced at the red-scripted embossed letters. "They're expecting me."

"Please wait here, Miss D'Enfer," she said in a soft accent, leading me into a parlor tastefully decorated with floral prints and dark furniture. The huge vase of magnolia blossoms was a allergist's nightmare.

She had barely walked out when the altercation across the hall started.

"Mo-*ther*!" a voice shrieked. "I will *not* have a curfew! You and your curfew can go to *hell*!" The final words were emphasized by the sound of shattering glass.

I couldn't help but smile. I had a real Scarlett O'Hara on my hands. Perfect.

WE SAT OUT ON THE BACK VERANDA, OVERLOOKING A LAWN that looked like a golf course. A sweating pitcher of mint julep, fresh mint floating on top, and glasses were brought out by another maid. I got the important detail right, anyway.

Mrs. Pointer-Ashe frowned ever so slightly (it would be impolite to be too obvious) as she delicately paged through the substantial contract, which was longer than she no doubt had expected. She'd want her husband to look it over and tell her if it was all right for her to sign, but he'd be angry that she bothered him with it. The father's job in these situations is to pay for the coming-out ball and puff up like a proud pheasant when his daughter is presented, not be distracted with trivial details.

Mrs. Pointer-Ashe had very big blonde hair and a figure (and mannerisms) that bespoke diet pills. Her lips and nails were fuchsia, with a hint of bleed around her mouth where lines were grooving her skin. She was probably already scheduled for a facelift—she'd time it so she'd be healed just in time for the coming-out ball. ("How young she looks," she'd want the guests to say. "Can you believe her daughter is the deb? They look like sisters.")

In contrast, Alexandria was naturally slim and, although her makeup was artfully applied, it was nearly invisible. The sheer gloss that glistened on her luscious young lips probably drove boys to steal their mother's cold cream and lock themselves in their bedrooms with their computers targeted to a porn site—and she knew it. Her green eyes were heavy-lidded, like Paris Hilton's, but I could tell it was an affectation: she wasn't languid and hadn't lost all of her common sense yet.

Then again, the whole point of a debutante ball was to snag the richest, most prominent, handsome eligible young bachelor available. Only *then* could she relax, just a little.

The nuptials would be postponed, of course, until after the deb graduated from a suitable college (Wellesley, perhaps, or U. Miss.). In this day and age, an education was considered of social import. If one was expected to serve on the board of directors of various charities, one at least needed sorority president experience.

"What does the contract say?" Alexandria asked me. Her mother hadn't thought of that, was still squinting helplessly at the fine print on the first page.

"It highlights what I'll do for you and what I expect of you in return," I said. "For your part, you will refrain from drinking and smoking." I saw her eyes flicker towards the mint julep in her glass. Apparently this habit didn't bother her mother. I continued.

"I require abstinence in all areas, actually." I phrased it delicately so Mrs. Pointer-Ashe wouldn't notice, although Alexandria knew exactly what I meant, because I saw the flare of her nostrils. I estimated she'd been having sex regularly since she was fifteen. "I will not tolerate tardiness. Your full attention and participation during our sessions is of the utmost imperative.

"In return, I will teach you the etiquette for any situation you could ever encounter. You may think you know etiquette now, but I will prove you wrong and teach you what you lack. After I'm through with you, you will be able to comport yourself correctly and effortlessly with the Queen of England, the Emperor of China, the President of these fine United States, or the Lord God himself. I will ensure, finally, that your coming out will be a night you will never, ever forget."

It wasn't a promise I made lightly, and it wasn't one I'd ever broken.

Alexandria's jade-green eyes lit up at my final statement. That was the most important thing to her, of course. Later, fitting in to society would become an obsession, but now, her deb ball was the focus of her life.

It was often more important than one's own wedding. The deb ball highlighted just the girl. Even though at a wedding, the bride was the focus of attention, with the groom being more someone to inspect for adequacy, the groom was still *there*, standing next to her, taking up a tiny corner of the spotlight.

In comparison, the escorts at a deb ball were pretty much invisible.

"It has to be perfect," she said. "*Perfect.*"

"In the end, that will be up to you," I said.

OF COURSE, SHE WAS ENTIRELY INCAPABLE OF FULFILLING the terms of the contract.

Contrary to what everyone thinks, the mothers don't choose me. I choose the deb each season. I'm looking for someone very specific. As I said before, the Scarlett O'Hara type. Spoiled, strong-willed, prone to tantrums and bucking authority. She'll follow societal commands—at least, on the outside, and fool everybody in the process—but she won't follow parental rules, or, often, mine.

I'd laid out a full, formal dinner service on their dining room table, which was large enough on which to stage the Battle of Gettysburg. When Alexandria saw the table setting, she heaved an elaborate sigh.

"I've already *done* this," she said, her voice almost slipping into full whine mode. "At Miss Miranda's Sch—"

I slammed my hand down on the table, causing the china, and Alexandria, to jump. The china clattered; Alexandria stayed silent, although her skin may have paled every so slightly.

"Miss Miranda," I said, "is a two-bit hack. Her methods are outdated, her knowledge is several years behind the times, and she graduates every deb who goes through her school, cultivated or not, because she's terrified of being ostracized by their families. Think about that, Miss Pointer-Ashe—are you sure you received accolades because you really learned everything you needed to know?"

She pressed her lips together, but I could tell I'd struck a nerve.

After our session, she would immediately is run out and tell everyone about Miss Miranda's. By being the first, she would thus negate the fact that her own education there might have been inadequate.

I rang a small silver bell, indicating that we should sit.

I corrected the placement of her napkin across her knees, questioned her deportment with the finger bowl, and pointed out any number of miniscule errors to catch her off guard. Then I quizzed her: tell me what every utensil is used for.

She was good, but when she got a particular cocktail fork, she hesitated. Of course she did. She'd never seen it before.

Alexandria frowned, turning the fork between her fingers. It was shaped like a small pitchfork.

"An...oyster fork?" she ventured.

"No." I picked up my own oyster fork and displayed it.

She pondered it for a while longer, and then threw it on the table.

"This is *so stu*pid!" she said. "I *hate* this! I will never, ever have to use all of this crap at a dinner!" She scraped her chair back, tossed her napkin on the floor in an even greater display of pique, and stomped towards the door.

"It is a fork," I said, "for eating hearts."

She turned, slowly, half-hypnotized by the sound of my voice, even though I hadn't raised it or changed the emotion in it.

"You're joking," she said.

"I never joke," I said.

"Then you're lying."

"Are you willing to take that chance?"

Alexandria hesitated.

I drove the final nail. "Zoe Cartwright Smith and Lucinda Matherson are coming out at a group ball."

She visibly shuddered. Coming out at a cotillion with other girls meant you didn't get the entire spotlight. It meant your father couldn't afford to throw you your own ball. It meant you and your family and your entire lineage were of substandard stock.

"You won't let that happen." She phrased it as a statement. So help me, she raised her chin and looked down her nose at me as she continued, "My father is paying you good money to ensure that doesn't happen. You *pro*mised."

It was all I could do not to laugh.

"I promised you that your coming out will be a night you will never forget, and I stand by that promise. But you must remember your end of the contract."

Alexandria pursed her glistening lips. I knew where those lips had been, what they had been wrapped around, just last night. She wasn't holding up her end of the contract at all, just as I expected.

"Very well," she said, falsely demure, and sat back down.

<hr>

SLOWLY, ALEXANDRIA GREW TO TRUST ME. OF COURSE, that meant that she exposed even more of her true nature to me. I've ducked a lot of flying crystal and flung vases in my day, and I have to say Alexandria was a connoisseur. She had an arm like Pedro Martinez and a temper like Mike Tyson. Or Scarlett, if you held to the true Southern ways. Scarlett is a goddess to them.

And so, when it was time for Alexandria to buy a dress (pure white, as prescribed, not ivory or pearl, with no ruffles or plunging neckline), it was me she turned to for advice. Mrs. Pointer-Ashe plucked at her own white gloves and gave comment, but as Alexandria came out of the dressing room and onto the short runway (it was one of those types of stores, of course), it was my approval she sought, my face her eyes turned to.

"That one's lovely," Mrs. Pointer-Ashe murmured.

"Alexandria, darling, I'm afraid that one makes you look like a two-bit whore," I called out. "Never, ever, go for a skirt like that in a formal dress. Cocktail dress, absolutely. But evening wear.... Not unless you're planning on standing on a street corner in the hopes that Bradley Winthrop the Third comes driving by."

On one hand, she would be coming out at her own private function. The dress would be unique. On the other hand, if anyone else within three counties had the same dress, her life would be ruined. *Ruined*, you understand. She might as well wear her dress from last year's Spring Cotillion. (Insert disgusted flounce here.)

She was getting tired. The latest dress was almost right, but not quite. I pointed out the inappropriateness of the silk rosette on the left shoulder.

"Gahd*damn*it!" She reached up, grasped the simple satin bodice, and ripped it cleanly down, revealing perky breasts most starlets would pay thousands for. She managed a few nicely pointed stomps on the skirt, which puddled around her new white satin pumps before she kicked it away and stormed back off to the dressing room.

Mrs. Pointer-Ashe looked stunned, or perhaps stoned, if I hadn't known her drugs of choice.

"I think this is going rather well, don't you?" I asked.

Then I sat, examining my blood-red nails, and waited.

Eventually, Alexandria came back out, looking rather meek.

"I'm sorry," she said. "That was undignified of me. I'll pay for that dress, of course."

Actually, Daddy would pay for it, but that wasn't the point.

I regarded her silently. The dress she was now wearing was ideal. Floor-length, always a requirement. No lace or elaborate beading, just a stiff satin bodice with cap sleeves and a sweetheart neckline, leading into a satin skirt overlaid with yards and yards of tulle.

"Thank you, Alexandria," I said. "A proper lady knows

when and how to apologize. Your mother and I accept your contrition."

This—the buying of the dress—was the final test. It proved I had her complete trust. She looked only to me for an opinion, never once glancing her mother's way, not even when I told her the dress was exquisite, perfect.

She would do anything I told her to do. As long as I was present. Behind my back, I knew she still had a long litany of contract violations to account for.

THE NIGHT OF ALEXANDRIA'S COMING-OUT BALL, I accompanied her in the limousine. Her parents would drive to the venue on their own. Once we were settled (carefully, so as to not crush her dress), I poured her a glass of champagne and toasted her success. Her dress was perfect. Her hair was exquisite. Her gloves and shoes were spotless. Her deportment was impeccable. She knew how to eat, dance, curtsy, make small talk, and gracefully remove herself from an awkward situation. She practically knew how not to sweat, even in the high summer Southern heat. That last one was going to come in particularly handy.

She hesitated, knowing she wasn't supposed to drink alcohol. I smiled encouragingly, and she took that as a sign that it was okay.

Encouraging smiles do not supercede a signed contract.

We finished the bottle (she never noticed that I never poured myself a second glass) and were down to the dregs of a second one when she passed out.

SHE AWOKE SEVERAL HOURS LATER, PRESSING A HAND TO her head and uttering a string of impressive oaths until she was coherent enough to remember I was there. She sat up and stared. The windowless bedroom was very red: wallpaper, silk sheets and bed canopy, carpet. This was not a room anywhere near the cotillion ballroom.

Then it began.

"Where am I? Where the fuck am I?" She flung herself at the door, but it was locked. She wrenched at the doorknob hard enough that even I feared it would break off. "What have you done? When my daddy finds me, he is going to—to —to fire you! And then he's going to have you thrown in jail! And he's not going to pay you anymore!"

She launched herself at me, but I stepped aside and she fell on the bed. The pillow became her next target; she screamed incoherently as she shredded it, spitting out the feathers that flurried around her.

Eventually she wore herself out, at which point I quietly said, "Alexandria."

I'd trained her well. She jumped and composed herself without thinking, then glared.

"You've made quite a mess of yourself, and we don't have much time to get you cleaned up. Luckily you haven't harmed your dress." I produced a brush and hairspray. "Hair first, then we'll touch up your makeup."

"Where am I?" she asked again.

"Hell," I said.

"You're crazy. Mother and Daddy put me in the hands of an insane person."

I pressed her down onto the stool in front of the vanity, and ran the brush through her hair.

"We had a contract, Alexandria. You signed it, openly and honestly, without coercion."

"You lied to me." Her voice was sullen.

I sprayed hairspray, then handed her some concealer. She dabbed it under her eyes.

"No, I didn't lie," I said. "The contract stipulated that you would refrain from drinking, smoking, and sexual activities. You failed on all accounts. It stated that you would comport yourself with dignity, and yet I endured tantrum after tantrum. It clearly outlined what would happen if you did not hold to the terms stated in the contract."

She stared at me in the mirror. Her mouth worked, but no sound came out. She hadn't read the contract. Neither had her parents. Alexandria and Mrs. Pointer-Ashe had signed it without checking any of the fine print.

I helped her to her feet.

"I didn't lie to you, Alexandria," I said as I opened the door. The smell of brimstone was stronger out here. "I promised you that your coming out will be a night you would never forget, and that is absolutely true."

Hand on her elbow, I guided her to the ballroom where every year, Satan held a cotillion, and charged me with obtaining him an appropriate debutante to present.

Alexandria balked in the doorway. The smell of brimstone was almost overpowering here, but like a true deb, she didn't complain—her expression didn't even change. I could sense His Fieryness near, eagerly waiting.

"I don't understand something," Alexandria said. Her gaze was on the room; her hand was poised on my arm as if I were her escort. "If a deb you've trained disappears every year, why doesn't anybody notice?"

"Honey, you're not stuck here forever," I said. "At least, not yet. When it's your time, He'll come for your soul. As far as the rest of the world will remember, you came out as the perfect deb, the most eligible young man in the county asked for your hand, and the night will be hailed as a true success."

"What will I remember?"

"Not a thing. You'll wake up tomorrow with the mother of all hangovers and—"

She whirled to face me, her dress rustling. "I won't remember?"

I shook my head.

"But..." A smile curved her glossy lips. "But you promised me a coming out I'd never forget. It was in the contract. *You* broke the contract. You never even intended to honor it."

A rumble shook the floor. Alexandria paled, but otherwise kept her composure. I recognized the sound: His laughter. I dropped to my knees.

"Your Eminence, I—"

"Too late, Lilith," He said. "She found a loophole. Absolutely delightful, my dear," He said to Alexandria. "You're the first one to catch that. Even I missed it." He held out His arm. "Come, my dear. After you're presented, we'll add a new tradition to the ball. Give you a chance to use that fork for hearts."

"You're going to kill Lilith?" she asked.

"Is that what you want?"

"Nooo..."

My head was still down, so all I saw was the hem of her skirt swish as she walked away.

"I think," Miss Alexandria Pointer-Ashe said, a charming lilt in her voice, "that it would be much more fun to do it while she's still alive."

* * *

Author's Note

THIS STORY WAS INSPIRED BY A CALL FOR SUBMISSIONS FOR an anthology about hell. Probably a funny anthology about hell; I no longer have the details. Certainly the story turned out pretty funny. Let's face it, debutantes are kinda silly, and the minute you make one nasty and pretentious, you've got comedy gold on your hands.

That said, I had no idea how the story was going to end, up until I got to the end. ::pats subconscious fondly:: I love it when a plan comes together. Mint juleps for everyone!

"Hell's Belles" appeared in *Deathgrip: Exit Laughing* (Hell-bound Books, 2006).

WHAT DRAGONS PREFER

I looked down from my horse at the mayor of this town I'd been sent to save, and wondered why I immediately found him so distasteful. Perhaps it was the fact that he had given to titling himself "Lord." Perhaps I was picking up clues from the townsfolk, particularly the women, who avoided him even as they crowded around me.

Or perhaps it was the way his eyes slid over me as he tried to see exactly what lay beneath my leather jerkin.

"Dragonslayer," he greeted, his smile slick beneath his well-oiled mustache. "Thank you for coming to aid us in our time of terror."

"I prefer 'Dragonseeker,'" I said politely. "It is not enough to have the skills to slay a dragon—one must learn about him as well. To know one's enemy is to destroy him."

And most people knew so little about dragons. I knew, for example, that dragons only fed once every twenty years, and then usually only one human. Is that such a bad thing, really, when wolves kill so many deer in the forest to survive, or humans kill sheep because roast mutton is so tasty? But people panicked if they saw a dragon glide far overhead on the highest currents, or if they caught a faint whiff of its acrid scent when the wind turned just right.

He insisted I spend the night in comfort at his home. I found something else to dislike: his manor was too opulent compared to the rest of the farming village, and had been built, no doubt, at the townsfolk's expense. It even had a rooftop garden!

"Do you lure the dragons with your virginity?" he asked during dinner.

"No," I said. I suspected he was less interested in how I lure dragons than in my possible virginal state. My supposition was confirmed when he muttered, "Pity," and turned his attentions to his meal.

I bolted the door to my room that night, and a good thing, for the latch rattled and I heard a thwarted curse.

I AROSE THE NEXT MORNING BEFORE DAWN AND BEFORE THE mayor, whom I doubted had seen a sunrise in many a year. I, on the other hand, knew that dragons are nocturnal, and would find this one sleeping when I reached its lair.

While I hastily ate a cold sausage roll and drank a cup of tea standing up in the kitchen, I asked his cook if the dragon had carried off many of the town's residents.

"Hardly likely," she snorted, slapping her fists into the bread dough. "His lordship makes sure each girl is 'protected,' as he says, barely a day past their first blooding."

The tea turned bitter on my tongue. So he thought ridding the town's young girls of their virginity would keep the dragon at bay? My instincts about him had been all too correct.

I rode off to find the dragon.

"All that's left is discussion of my payment," I told him when I returned the next evening. When I suggested we hold the discussion in his rooftop garden, his smile grew far too broad.

I had barely tucked the purse in my belt and dodged his first advance when the dragon arrived for her 20-year meal.

Another thing few people know about dragons is that while the males prefer female virgins, the females like their men experienced.

Know your enemies, indeed.

Author's Note

It seems fitting to end this collection with my first professionally published story. I'm terribly fond of this one for a number of reasons. Yes, it's very short—but I believe it's just as long as it needs to be, to say what it has to say.

I'm extremely proud of the fact that I sold it to a magazine editor who always said in their guidelines that dragon stories were a very hard sell for them. Not only that, but the story won third place in the "Cauldron Awards" that ran in every issue of the magazine (for the previous issue's stories, voted on by readers).

I wanted to leave you with a smile on your face, and I hope this story fits the bill.

"What Dragons Prefer" originally appeared in *Marion Zimmer Bradley's Fantasy Magazine*, Fall 1994 (Issue 25). And if you want to hear it read aloud, head on over to Podcastle.org (2008)!

ALSO BY DAYLE A. DERMATIS

NOVELS

The Nikki Ashburne Novels

Ghosted

Shaded (forthcoming)

Spectered (forthcoming)

Beautiful Beast

Waking the Witch

What Beck'ning Ghost

COLLECTIONS

Devilish Deals and Perilous Pacts: A Spooky Collection of Deals With the Devil and Other Bad Choices

Five Funny Fantasies

Haunted (a Nikki Ashburne collection, forthcoming)

Small Wonders: Ten Short-Short Speculative Fiction Stories

Umberto Scolari and the Five Mysteries: A Short Story Collection

Voices Carry and Other Stories of Women and Crime

Written on the Coast: Thirteen Stories of Magic and Mayhem Written in Lincoln City, OR

NONFICTION

Researching History for Fantasy Writers: How to Use Historical Detail to Make Your Fantasy Worlds Rich and Compelling

ABOUT THE AUTHOR

Dayle A. Dermatis is the author or coauthor of many novels (including snarky urban fantasies *Ghosted* and the forthcoming *Shaded* and *Spectered*) and more than a hundred short stories in multiple genres, appearing in such venues as *The Saturday Evening Post*, *Alfred Hitchcock's Mystery Magazine*, and DAW Books.

Called the mastermind behind the *Uncollected Anthology* project, she also guest edits anthologies for *Fiction River*, and her own short fiction has been lauded in many year's best anthologies in erotica, mystery, and horror.

She lives in a book- and cat-filled historic English-style cottage in the wild greenscapes of the Pacific Northwest. In her spare time she follows Styx around the country and travels the world, which inspires her writing.

To find out where she's wandered off to (and to get free fiction!), check out DayleDermatis.com and sign up for her newsletter or support her on Patreon.

I value honest feedback, and would love to hear your opinion in a review, if you're so inclined, on your favorite book retailer's site.

For more information:
www.dayledermatis.com

BE THE FIRST TO KNOW!

Sign up for Dayle A. Dermatis's newsletter for *free* fiction, plus the latest news, releases, and more.

Sign up at DayleDermatis.com.

For more in-depth conversations and special sneak peeks, you can also support her continued work by joining her community of patrons out Dayle's Patreon.

Patreon.com/Dayle